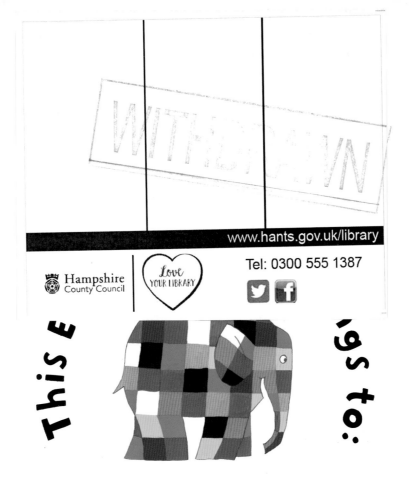

To Enid Willow

This paperback edition first published in Great Britain in 2018 by Andersen Press Ltd.
First published in Great Britain in 2017 by Andersen Press Ltd.,
20 Vauxhall Bridge Road, London SW1V 2SA.
Copyright © David McKee, 2017.
The right of David McKee to be identified as the author and
illustrator of this work has been asserted by him in accordance
with the Copyright, Designs and Patents Act, 1988.
All rights reserved.
Colour separated in Switzerland by Photolitho AG, Zürich.
Printed and bound in Malaysia.

1   3   5   7   9   10   8   6   4   2

British Library Cataloguing in Publication Data available.

ISBN 978 1 78344 593 6

"Good morning, Elmer," said Lion.
"I like that tune you're humming."
"I got it from Rose," said Elmer.
"Now I can't stop humming it."
Elmer went on his way and Lion
started humming the tune.

A little later Elmer met Hippo. Hippo was also
humming the tune.

"Hello, Hippo," said Elmer. "I hear that Rose came by."

"How did you know?" asked Hippo.

"The tune," said Elmer, going on his way. "The tune."

Further along, Elmer thought he heard the tune coming from the lake.

"That's strange," he thought and put his head under the water. There was Crocodile bubbling Rose's tune. With a laugh Elmer bubbled along with Crocodile for a moment before carrying on his walk.

Elmer was still humming when he heard Tiger.
"Hello Tiger," he said. "I think you've seen Rose."
"No," said Tiger in surprise. "Why do you say that?"
"The tune you're humming," said Elmer.
"Oh that," said Tiger. "When I passed Lion he was
humming it. Now I can't stop."

He'd just left Tiger when Elmer heard the tune coming from above him. The monkeys were humming together.

"Incredible," thought Elmer. "We're all humming Rose's tune. I think I'll have a quiet nap to get it out of my head."

Elmer was woken from his quiet nap by the sound of loud talking. The tune was still in his head as he went to see what was going on.

"Hello Elmer," said Lion. "We have a problem. It's the tune – we can't get it out of our heads."

"Me too," said Elmer. "I have an idea. Do any of you have a birthday today?" Nobody did. "Well, somebody somewhere does. Let's sing 'Happy Birthday' together."

"All right, Elmer," said Tiger. "But you are funny."

They started singing, timidly at first, but getting stronger and stronger as they went on.
"Happy birthday to you, happy birthday to you. Happy birthday dear somebody, happy birthday to you."

"Again and louder," said Elmer as Rose arrived and joined in. When they had finished the second time he said, "And again."

They all sang it a third and fourth time, stopped and burst out laughing.

"It worked," said Crocodile. "The tune has gone. Thanks, Elmer." Everyone echoed his words. "Thanks, Elmer." "Thanks, Elmer."

As the others went their various ways, Rose said, "I wonder whose birthday it was?"

A few days later Lion and Tiger came by.
"Hello Elmer," said Lion. "We're trying to
remember that tune. How did it go again?"
"I've forgotten," said Elmer.
"Pity," said Tiger. "It was a catchy little number."
And they left.

When they'd gone, the elephants roared with laughter.
"Well, I didn't want to start that again," said Elmer.

"But you'd think they'd know by now:
an elephant never forgets."
"You are naughty, Elmer," said an elephant. Then, still
laughing, they chased him all the way home.

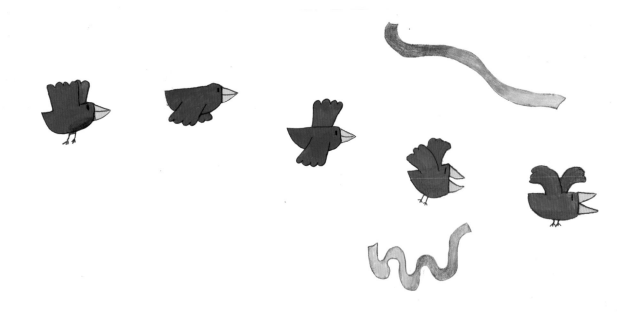